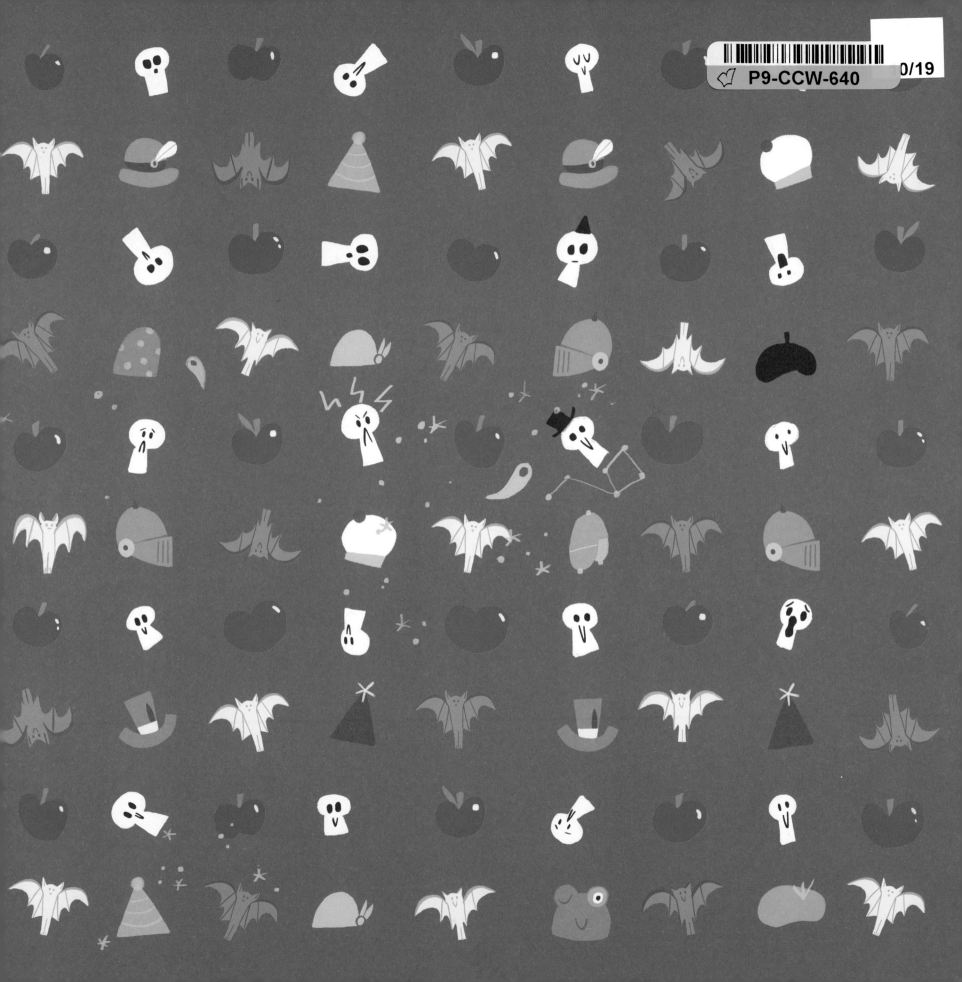

To my parents, and to Mercedes

First U.S. edition 2019

Library of Congress Catalog Card Number 2018962230
ISBN 978-1-5362-0572-5

19 20 21 22 23 24 TLF 10 9 8 7 6 5 4 3 2

Printed in Dongguan, Guangdong, China

This book was typeset in Graham.
The illustrations were created digitally.

TEMPLAR BOOKS

an imprint of
Candlewick Press
99 Dover Street
Somerville, Massachusetts 02144
www.candlewick.com

THE RIGHT ONE FOR RODERIC

Violeta Noy

templar books

an imprint of Candlewick Press

Roderic was the smallest ghost
in the largest family that had ever
lived through the centuries.

You might wonder why all the ghosts in
Roderic's family look the same: it's the white sheets.
That's what ghosts always wear. And Roderic
wore the smallest white sheet of all.

He was also the last in a long line of Roderics . . .

which made him feel even smaller.

Most of the time, Roderic felt like his family
didn't notice he was there.

Especially when his aunts
floated right through him.

Maybe they don't see me, Roderic thought.
But that could be fixed, right?

If he couldn't change his name and couldn't change his family, perhaps he could change how he looked.

He started small
and tried on a hat.

It didn't seem like much,
so he tried on another . . .

and another . . .

and another.

Roderic thought he looked fantastic, distinguished even,
but as soon as he started moving, the hats all flew away.

Perhaps a scarf? he thought next.
But that didn't work either.

The next morning he got bolder and put on a poncho instead of his usual white sheet.

The colors were great, even though his ectoplasm (that's what ghosts are made of) kept showing.

Then he added back some hats . . .

a shorter scarf . . .

and a bow tie.

Finally, Roderic was ready
to show off his new look.

But when he appeared at breakfast,
things didn't go the way he'd planned.

His aunts didn't like his outfit . . . .

and his parents
didn't approve.

Roderic thought that maybe
the castle wasn't the
place for him.

So he drifted to the city,
where he hoped everyone would
have better fashion sense.

When he got there, he waited for
people to notice his elegant clothes.

They didn't even see him.

Soon he felt even more
lost and invisible than
he had at home.

His family had gone looking for him, but when they finally found him,
Roderic had lost his beautiful outfit. They hugged and kissed
him and took him home.

They told him they had the perfect thing for him to wear.

But it was just another white sheet.

Roderic was not happy.
The sheet still felt wrong,
so he tried on some new things.

then a handbag
(his mom got
soooo mad),

First, he put on a rug
(it was dusty and
made him sneeze),

then a tablecloth
(it made him smell
like peas),

and even a shower curtain
(which just made him damp).

Nothing felt right.

A BAT

A SHEET →

GRANDMA'S FAVORITE SKULL

It was SO FRUSTRATING!
When ghosts get emotional, things start to fly around.
And Roderic was feeling very emotional.

SLIME

GRANDMA'S SECOND
FAVORITE SKULL

A BONE

A BOOT

Furniture fell over, cupboards flew open,
and things that had been lost
appeared again . . .

just like the thing that landed on Roderic's head.

It smelled and
swished like his
old sheet . . .

but this one felt much, much better.

As soon as Roderic looked in
the mirror, he knew this was
the right one.

He went to show his family, and this time
he had something very important to say to them:

And you know what?
Everybody loved it!

Because even though Roderic was
the smallest ghost in the largest family
that had ever lived through the centuries . . .

that didn't mean he couldn't
teach them a thing or two.

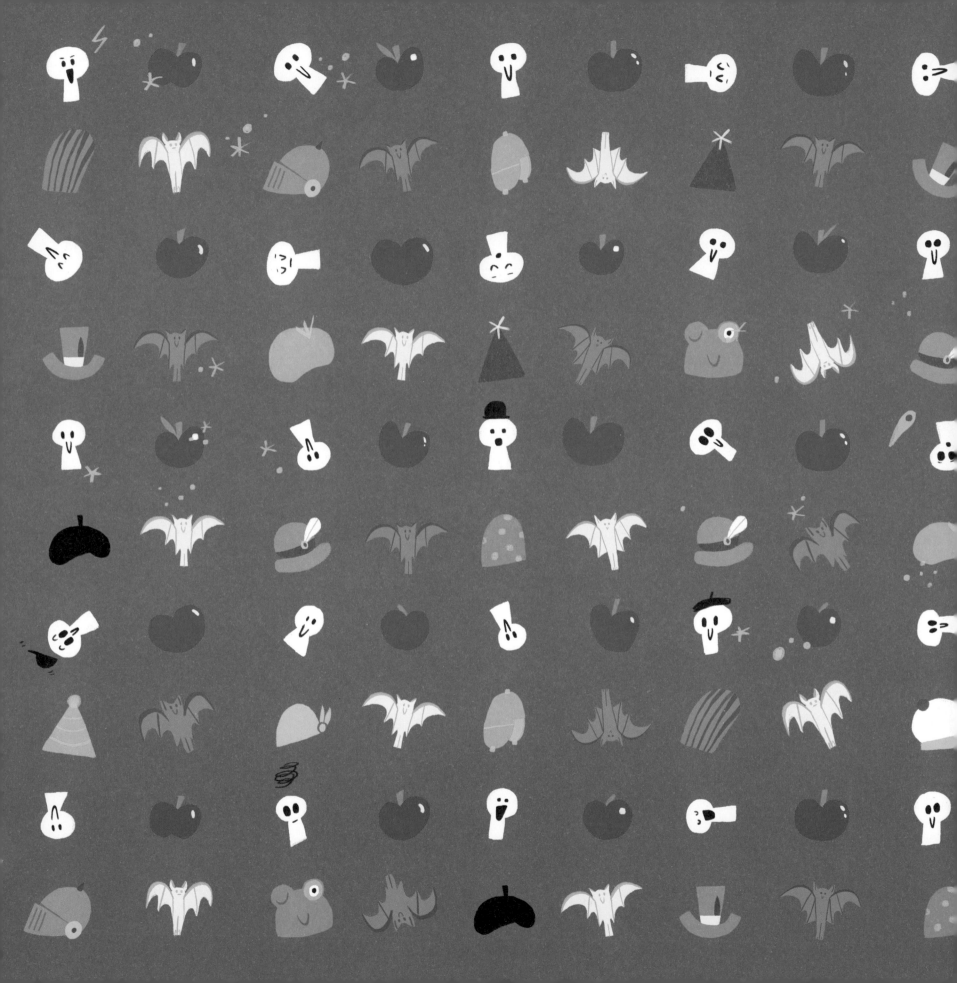